MW00904981

Mirror Game

Dennis Foon

Playwrights Canada Press
Toronto • Canada

Playwrights Canada Press
The Canadian Drama Publisher
215 Spadina Avenue, Suite 230, Toronto, Ontario CANADA M5T 2C7
416-703-0013   fax 416-408-3402
orders@playwrightscanada.com • www.playwrightscanada.com

Financial support provided by the taxpayers of Canada and Ontario through the Canada Council for the Arts and the Department of Canadian Heritage through the Book Publishing Industry Development Programme, and the Ontario Arts Council.

Cover design by Jodi Armstrong.

National Library of Canada Cataloguing in Publication Data

Foon, Dennis, 1951-
    Mirror game / Dennis Foon.

A play.
Originally published: Winnipeg : Blizzard Pub., 1992.
ISBN 0-88754-654-4

    I. Title.

PS8561.O62M5 2002   C812'.54   C2002-903693-3
PR9199.3.F5667M57 2002

Printed August 2002. Second Printing: August 2006.
Printed and bound by Canadian Printco at Scarborough, Canada.

A one-act version of *Mirror Game*, suitable for school touring, was first produced by Green Thumb Theatre on tour in British Columbia in February–June 1988 with the following cast:

BOB	Wayne Yorke
SARA	Lorna Olafson
MAGGIE	Jill Daum
LUKE	Peter Giaschi

Directed by Dennis Foon
Designed by Daniel Castonguay
Stage Managed by Kenn Walker

Copies of that script are available from the Playwrights Union of Canada. This two-act version was first produced by Young People's Theatre, Toronto, February 27, 1991 with the following cast:

BOB	Oliver Dennis
SARA	Deborah Drakeford
MAGGIE	Alison Sealy-Smith
LUKE	Hamish McEwan
MR.MOSS/TEACHER	Richard Sacks

Directed by Richard Greenblat
Music composed and performed by Richard Sacks
Set and Costumes designed by Teresa Przbylski
Lighting designed by Stephan Droege
Choreographed by Susan McKenzie
Stage Managed by Melissa Veal

Acknowledgements

This expanded version of the play, commissioned by Young People's Theatre, owes much to the director, Richard Greenblat, and the May 1990 workshop company: Ted Dykstra, Kyra Harper, Alison Sealy-Smith and Jim Warren.

I would also like to thank Janet Freeman and Debra J. Lewis at the Vancouver Battered Women's Support Services for their advice and support.

Special thanks to Judith Hogan and her Grade Twelve drama class at Gladstone High School for giving so generously of their time and themselves. This play is dedicated to them: Alex, Sheila, Lina, Belinda, Paddy, Vir, Sandy, Mike, Lara, Geraldine, Cindy and Bill.

Characters

BOB
SARA
MAGGIE
LUKE
THEIR PARENTS
(who are never seen in full view, but who appear as shadows)
MR. MOSS
(a teacher, also off stage)

The play may be performed by four actors.

The Set

The play takes place in a wide range of areas. It is not necessary to represent these areas naturalistically. The basic requirement is a large screen, so the adults may appear as shadows. It may also be useful to demarcate "home" areas for each of the kids.

The Shadows

The adults are portrayed as shadow figures, projections of the teens' points of view. My hope is to create an expressionistic feeling for the parents and to leave a great deal of room for experimentation in the staging.

It is crucial to clearly differentiate each set of parents, both vocally and in silhouette. To give you an idea of how they may be presented, here are some examples from Richard Greenblat's production:

Bob's dad sat in a chair with a cigar and a remote control, with Bob's mother hovering over him. Maggie's mother was the profile of a woman in a chair, holding a drink. Joe and Mary (Sara's mother and boyfriend) were shown in full, with Joe circling around Mary. At the end of the play, as Sara moved away from Luke, Mary came closer and closer to Joe until on the line, "I only have you," she appeared to merge into him.

Richard also used a fascinating blend of front and rear projection. In one scene, Luke's father appeared behind the screen. Luke stood in front and faced the screen, his shadow projected much smaller, giving us the impression of Luke as a young boy. After Luke was beaten down, his shadow grew and grew, taking over the place of his father's shadow.

Given different resources and imaginations, I am sure many other approaches to the shadows will be used in subsequent productions.

The Action

The action of the play is meant to be continuous. It is not necessary to have an interval between the acts.

On Casting

The students whose stories inspired *Mirror Game* had diverse ancestries. It is my hope that this play be cast multi-racially in order to accurately reflect their lives and our society. In particular, the role of Maggie should be played by a person of colour.

Act One

(The lights come up on BOB, who is looking at himself in the mirror. He speaks to the audience.)

BOB: Well, here we go. Another one. I hate zits. I hate them! But they like me, they keep coming back. At least somebody likes you, Bob. The reason I have so many zits is 'cause my head's too big. So much skin, they can't resist it. Oh, God, look at this one. I gotta squeeze it, gotta squeeze it—no stop! Don't, it'll just get huge and red and infected and ooze yellow pus—I'm gonna cut my fingers off! It's the only way not to squeeeeeze.

(BOB stands on his hands. Bob's DAD is heard, off.)

DAD: Bobby!

(BOB freezes, indicates that the audience should remain quiet.)

Bobby, have you seen the TV guide?

MOM: Your stupid TV guide's on top of your stupid TV!

(BOB listens. Pause. BOB exhales.)

BOB: Most people I know don't have these problems. Take my friend Maggie, for example. Her life is perfect.

(Lights on MAGGIE, who drags herself out of bed.)

She has all this energy, practically runs the school, gets all A's and she's in incredible physical condition.

(MAGGIE steps on the scale, sees the weight and grimaces.)

It's because of her completely positive attitude, I guess.

(MAGGIE steps off the scale, removes her slippers, steps back on the scale, looks hopefully at the result.)

Nothing ever gets her down.

(*MAGGIE sees the weight and sadly shakes her head.*)

She is a bit of a hippie, though. She's always trying to get me to join one of her environmental or political groups. She's real peace and love.

(*MAGGIE quickly does some martial arts moves, a series of deadly punches.*)

You know what I mean? But I figure, whatever makes you happy.

(*Satisfied, MAGGIE steps back on the scale, checking the result. She sighs, defeated, and faces the mirror. As BOB puts a bandaid on his zit, his DAD is heard, off.*)

DAD: Bobby! What are you doing up there?

BOB: Nothing!

DAD: (*Almost singing.*) There's something going ahh-on!

BOB: (*Mimicking him.*) No there's nahhh-ot!

DAD: You've been in that bathroom for over an hour!

BOB: Squatters' rights!

DAD: Are you in there with someone?

BOB: I only wish! (*To audience.*) It's easy to make jokes about it, but I'll probably die of terminal virginity. Maybe I set my sights too high. Maybe I can't see at all. But there's this girl, Sara. And she's the most beautiful, perfect—

(*Romantic music starts and then is cut off abruptly by MOM's voice.*)

MOM: What are you doing in there?

BOB: Nothing!

MOM: Are you doing your homework?

BOB: Yes!

MOM: Don't lie to me!

DAD: Ruth, leave the boy alone!

MOM: Do you want him to fail?

DAD: You won't fail, will you, Bobby?

BOB: No, Dad.

MOM: What a father! His son's flunking out, and he just sits there.

DAD: At least I'm not badgering him to death!

MOM: He needs to be badgered if he's gonna do something with his life!

DAD: Do you want to do something with your life, Bobby?

BOB: Yes, Dad.

DAD: See? Oop, halftime's over, back to the game.

MOM: He's gonna be a loser just like you.

DAD: Do you want to be a loser, Bobby?

BOB: No, Dad.

MOM: Don't worry, you will!

BOB: Thanks a lot, Mom.

MOM: You're welcome!

(*Romantic music starts again. BOB to audience.*)

BOB: Sara. Sara. She doesn't walk, she kinda floats. She doesn't talk, she kinda sings.

(*SARA enters, crossing angelically behind BOB.*)

The words vibrate and go right through my ears and I just start shaking all over. And her smile and those white teeth, I feel like the ice is just melting off me. And her touch? Like floating in a warm tropical pool. I've never floated in a warm tropical pool but I'm sure that's what it's like.

(*SARA starts putting some makeup on. MAGGIE enters, out of breath.*)

MAGGIE: Oh God, I don't think he saw me. Do you think he saw me?

SARA: Mr. Wallis? He won't do anything even if he did.

MAGGIE: I've never skipped out of a test before.

SARA: It doesn't even count for marks, Maggie.

MAGGIE: I know, but still ...

SARA: Self-esteem: Give ten reasons why you like yourself.

MAGGIE: Some test.

SARA: I had to get out of there, Maggie, it was too stupid.

MAGGIE: Not only that, I was going to have to sit next to The Tweezle.

SARA: Did you know after he picks his nose, he rolls them up into little balls and saves them for snacks?

MAGGIE: That's gross.

SARA: Oh, I don't know, I hear they contain lots of Vitamin C.

(*The girls freeze.*)

BOB: She's so wise and intelligent and perceptive. The first time she spoke to me, I thought she was talking to somebody else.

(*MAGGIE exits with a wave to SARA. SARA sees BOB.*)

SARA: Is your name Bob?

BOB: Bob? Me? No. I mean yes. Yes.

(*SARA laughs.*)

BOB: (*To audience.*) Oh my God.

SARA: Do you have Mr. Kweeg in math?

BOB: Yes, yes. Yes, I do.

SARA: Did he give you the quiz yesterday?

BOB: Yes. Oh he did, yeah.

SARA: Do I need to read chapters five and six?

BOB: No, no, it's really easy.

SARA: Oh, good, that's a relief.

BOB: Yeah ... do you want to know some of the questions?

SARA: No, that's okay.

BOB: I can help you.

SARA: That's nice of you.

BOB: Is something wrong with your arm?

SARA: No, I tripped last night and fell.

BOB: Oh no.

SARA: I was up so late I forgot to study.

BOB: Well, I can coach you. I'll give you the questions.

SARA: You're sweet.

(*She squeezes his hand. Music from heaven. BOB turns to the audience and does a few leaps of joy.*)

BOB: (*To audience.*) She touched me. I can't believe it. The most beautiful girl in the whole school, in the whole city, in the whole solar system likes me.

(*He smells where she touched him.*)

Perfume. Flowers. Nectar of Venus.

(He licks it.)

She loves me. I have a future. I have somebody. I have her. True love.

SARA: I was up late with my boyfriend last night.

BOB: Your boyfriend?

SARA: Luke. You know him? Drives the black Camaro?

BOB: Luke. Luke with the arms?

SARA: Arms? Oh, yeah, he lifts weights.

(BOB looks at audience, feels his biceps, shrugs.)

BOB: Yeah, I know who you're talking about. You been with him a long time?

SARA: Oh yeah, forever. Going on six months.

BOB: That's a long time.

SARA: Not when you're in love.

BOB: *(To audience.)* Even if your dreams are crushed, there's still hope. *(To SARA.)* Do you guys fight?

SARA: Fight? No. Not really. Not like other people.

BOB: *(To audience.)* Can't blame me for trying.

(LUKE enters.)

SARA: You should have seen me when I first met him. It was like he could read my mind.

LUKE: You feel like you're drowning. Like you can't breathe.

SARA: What?

LUKE: Everything's smothering you. You're being crushed by everybody, by the world.

SARA: How'd you know that?

LUKE: I just looked in your eyes. Look in mine. *(Pause.)* You can see it, can't you? We're the same. Our souls are crossed. Do you feel it?

SARA: ... I feel like ... I've known you ... forever.

LUKE: You have. And I've known you.

SARA: But why now ...?

LUKE: All we can do is grab onto it.

(They kiss. LUKE exits.)

BOB: That's really uh ... different.

SARA: *(To BOB.)* I can be ten miles away and he knows what I'm thinking. He knows me better than I know myself.

BOB: You're lucky.

SARA: You think so?

BOB: Oh yeah. Luckier than me.

SARA: Oh, Bob, you're sweet.

(She kisses him on the cheek and goes. BOB touches his cheek.)

BOB: *(To audience.)* Well, it beats getting kissed by my Aunt Bertha. But Luke? She really kisses him, she really loves him. Luke the Puke. But I can't get it out of my head. What's so great about this guy anyway? What's he got that I don't—besides biceps?

(LUKE runs on with a football.)

LUKE: Hey—wanna throw it around?

BOB: Me? Sure.

LUKE: Okay, 6-45 right.

BOB: ... Okay.

(BOB crouches in the hike position. Slight pause. BOB stands up.)

Uh, what's 6-45 right?

LUKE: Run six yards and cut 45 to the right.

BOB: Oh, yards—I thought you might mean metres.

LUKE: Paces.

BOB: Paces. No sweat.

(BOB hikes it to LUKE, runs six paces and cuts to the right. LUKE throws it on the money. BOB manages to catch it.)

LUKE: Nice catch. This time cut two to the left.

(BOB does, catches it.)

Hey, good hands.

BOB: No, you're just throwing it good. Are you on the team?

LUKE: No, don't have time. How about you?

BOB: Me on the team? Uh, no, I'm, uh, too busy—besides, football, I got better things to do.

LUKE: *(Smiles.)* I know what you mean ... My name's Luke.

BOB: Bob.

LUKE: See that guy over there—

BOB: The guy with the green hair?

LUKE: No, not Frank, the other guy.

BOB: The short one?

LUKE: Yeah, The Tweezle. We got him drunk for the first time last weekend.

BOB: Oh yeah?

LUKE: He drinks six beer and starts walking into street lamps and the whole time he's saying, "Am I drunk? Is this drunk? No, I must be pretending to be drunk."

BOB: Was he?

LUKE: I wasn't sure. But then he takes his clothes off, climbs a telephone pole, yells "Holy Water!" and drains his pickle all over the road.

BOB: I think he was drunk.

LUKE: He didn't think so. Later on, he stands on top of this jungle gym, yelling: "I'm not drunk, it's the flu! I'm just pretending." And then he pukes his guts out.

BOB: He was definitely drunk.

LUKE: Definitely. So how about it?

BOB: What?

LUKE: We're goin' out next Friday, wanna come?

BOB: Me?

LUKE: Yeah, I'll score the brew, Bob—how much you in for, a case?

BOB: Sure, it's just ... I gotta work.

LUKE: You got a weekend night shift?

BOB: Uh huh.

LUKE: That sucks.

BOB: That's life.

LUKE: Hey, don't worry about it, Bob. Next time.

BOB: Next time.

> (*LUKE points at BOB, BOB points back. LUKE exits. BOB shoots himself with the outstretched finger.*)

Okay, so he's a nice guy, great athlete, no zits, mega muscles and looks to kill. I don't get what Sara sees in him.

   (MAGGIE enters.)

MAGGIE: I can't believe you, Bob. The earth is dying and all you can think about is this ... female.

BOB: Maggie, she is no female! I mean ... she's a, a ... goddess.

MAGGIE: And she's been going out with Luke for six months. How can you be so out of it? She's your fantasy. And it's people and their stupid fantasies that are killing the world.

BOB: Who cares if the world dies, I got nothing to live for anyway.

MAGGIE: You've got plenty to live for.

BOB: Nobody loves me.

MAGGIE: There are some people who love you.

BOB: Yeah, like who?

MAGGIE: Like you know who.

BOB: Like you know who who?

MAGGIE: *(Covering.)* Like ... your parents.

BOB: Oh, them. They do?

MAGGIE: Don't they?

BOB: Well, they don't count. I'm talking about real love.

MAGGIE: Do you mean love or do you mean sex, Bob?

BOB: I'll take both.

MAGGIE: Same here. The Big Two.

BOB: ... God, it doesn't make any sense, does it, Maggie?

MAGGIE: What?

BOB: I mean, here we are, you and me.

MAGGIE: What about it?

BOB: We're friends, we can talk about anything.

MAGGIE: That's right.

BOB: We have something very special, very different.

MAGGIE: ... I know.

BOB: It seems really stupid that we don't get together, doesn't it?

   (Pause. She's been waiting a long time for this.)

MAGGIE: You think so? ... You mean like for the Big Two?

BOB: Well, yeah.

MAGGIE: ... Really?

BOB: Of course ... the problem is we're not in love with each other.

MAGGIE: *(Crushed.)* I guess not. I guess that's why we're just friends.

BOB: Yeah, right. Though sometimes I imagine kissing you.

MAGGIE: You do?

BOB: It's just like kissing a waffle.

MAGGIE: Thanks a lot.

BOB: Come on, Maggie, I don't mean like that. I love waffles. After all, one man's waffle is another man's ...

MAGGIE: Toilet paper.

BOB: Look, I'm sorry.

MAGGIE: It's alright.

BOB: I'm being a real jerk.

MAGGIE: I don't know why I hang around you anyway.

BOB: I know.

MAGGIE: You're a totally self-centred neurotic mess.

BOB: It's true.

MAGGIE: You're more worried about your pimples than acid rain.

BOB: I'm a mess.

MAGGIE: And you're having a spaz attack over somebody who's in love with somebody else.

BOB: Maggie, get off my back!

MAGGIE: Why do we have so much in common!

(She jumps on BOB's back. BOB exits with MAGGIE holding on, feet dragging behind.)

Home, James!

(SARA enters.)

SARA: Mom—Joe?

(MARY and JOE are seen as large shadows behind a screen, voices amplified.)

JOE: You got any money?

SARA: Yeah, why?

JOE: I want you to buy some cigarettes.

SARA: You're a big boy, pick them up yourself.

JOE: We put a roof over your head. We feed your butt.

SARA: My mom pays all the bills around here, not you.

JOE: You got a job, contribute!

MARY: That's her money for school, Joe.

JOE: Well, we gotta have money, too, don't we?

MARY: We do. I make enough for both of us. Just leave her out of it.

JOE: Oh, so now it's my fault, eh? I can't pull my weight, eh?

MARY: I didn't say that.

JOE: I heard what you said.

SARA: Get your ears cleaned.

JOE: Shut up!

MARY: Joe, please.

SARA: It's my house, I can say whatever the hell I want.

JOE: Mary, you stink, you know that?

SARA: Take a whiff of yourself sometime.

JOE: Why don't you ever wash?

MARY: I just got back from work.

JOE: I bet you were at work. Making eyes at your boss again.

MARY: No, I wasn't, Joe.

JOE: If I ever catch you with him, I'll kill you!

SARA: Oh great, Round Two.

(*All exit. MAGGIE and BOB enter, talking on the telephone.*)

BOB: Oh, come on, Maggie, you know her, you gotta help me.

MAGGIE: No, I do not have to help you.

BOB: All you have to do is tell her.

MAGGIE: Tell her what?

BOB: How I feel.

MAGGIE: You mean like, "Hi Sara, nice day, isn't it? By the way, Bob wants to jump your bones."

BOB: I do not!

MAGGIE: Oh, right, you wanna feel the magic.

BOB: She means more to me than that. That's not what it's all about.

MAGGIE: Well, if you just want to worship her, what do you need me for? Go to church!

BOB: I want to know if she feels anything for me.

MAGGIE: So ask her yourself.

BOB: I can't. I get too nervous. I might start compulsively belching.

MAGGIE: ... You should try it. I heard burping can be an aphrodisiac.

BOB: Please, Maggie. Just talk to her.

MAGGIE: Do you realize what you're asking me to do?

BOB: If you do it, I'll do anything for you, I'll join Greenpeace.

MAGGIE: Bob, you're a goof, you know that? If you're gonna do something to help the world it's got to come out of you, it shouldn't be a bribe. The planet we live on is dying, don't you care?

BOB: I'll join Greenpeace and your Top Choice group.

MAGGIE: That's Pro Choice, idiot!

BOB: I knew that.

MAGGIE: And you'll go on the Peace March?

BOB: For sure. Deal?

MAGGIE: ... Deal.

BOB: I love you!

    (BOB hangs up.)

MAGGIE: Screw you, Bob.

    (She hangs up. Maggie's MOTHER appears behind screen.)

MOTHER: When did you get home, Maggie?

MAGGIE: Just now, Mom. Where's Dad?

MOTHER: Away.

MAGGIE: Again? He was just out of town last week.

MOTHER: That's his job, darling.

MAGGIE: He's never here.

MOTHER: I know.

MAGGIE: Any news from Patty?

MOTHER: No news.

MAGGIE: Mom—let's say you really like somebody but they don't care, they like somebody else. Do you know what I mean? *(Pause.)* Mom?

MOTHER: What?

MAGGIE: What do you do if you love somebody but they don't love you?

MOTHER: Why are you asking me that question?

MAGGIE: Who else can I ask?

MOTHER: I don't know. But don't ask me.

MAGGIE: Mom—what is it?

MOTHER: I don't want to talk about it.

> *(MOTHER exits.)*

MAGGIE: Mom? ... Mom?

> *(Pause. MAGGIE picks up her school work, looks at it, then throws it down. SARA enters, goes into the washroom, lights a cigarette, starts working on her homework. MAGGIE goes to her.)*

Whatcha doing, Sara?

SARA: What's it look like?

> *(SARA offers MAGGIE a drag of her cigarette. MAGGIE tries it and coughs, hands it back.)*

MAGGIE: Is that your English assignment?

SARA: Yeah. I didn't get it done last night.

MAGGIE: I did it. Wanna copy it?

SARA: That's okay, I'm just about finished.

> *(Slight pause. SARA takes MAGGIE's assignment and copies it.)*

God, I don't believe I missed this one.

> *(They hear MR. MOSS's amplified voice.)*

MR. MOSS: *(Off.)* Do I smell cigarettes in there?

SARA: Not in here, Mr. Moss.

MR. MOSS: *(Off.)* Then just what are you doing?

SARA: I'm having a really bad period, sir.

MR. MOSS: *(Off.)* What?

SARA: Cramps, sir. Blood!

MR. MOSS: *(Off.)* I see. Well then, carry on. Good luck! B-bye.

SARA: Bye.

(The girls laugh.)

MAGGIE: You got guts, I wish I could do that.

SARA: Works every time.

MAGGIE: You're smart.

SARA: No, you're the one with brains.

MAGGIE: What else am I going to do but study? Every night of my life I'm sitting at home.

SARA: I wouldn't mind that. Home's the last place I ever want to be.

MAGGIE: Why?

SARA: My mom has this boyfriend.

MAGGIE: Yeah, so?

SARA: They fight all the time.

MAGGIE: They do?

SARA: Yeah, doesn't everybody?

MAGGIE: Mine don't.

SARA: Perfect life, eh?

MAGGIE: I mean, my dad's never home … he's away all the time on business.

SARA: My mom's last boyfriend was a businessman, really into golf. He was okay till he started drinking. One day he came home and broke all the windows in the house with his putter.

MAGGIE: You mean with his …?

SARA: Not that, it's a golf club, stupid.

MAGGIE: Good thing, that woulda hurt.

SARA: Yeah, I guess it woulda.

(They laugh.)

MAGGIE: Why don't you go live with your dad?

SARA: No, I can't, they took me and my brother away from him … I can't. Besides, I'll be moving out soon. I'll be on my own, right? See? Counting the days.

(SARA shows MAGGIE her arm.)

MAGGIE: What are those marks?

SARA: Cigarette burns. Seventeen. One for each year.

MAGGIE: Did you do that?

SARA: Yeah.

MAGGIE: Doesn't it hurt?

SARA: It's not that bad.

MAGGIE: God, Sara, why did you do it?

SARA: I felt like it.

MAGGIE: You must've been upset.

SARA: I've felt worse.

MAGGIE: What do you do when you feel worse?

SARA: I think about killing myself.

MAGGIE: You do?

(SARA nods yes.)

MAGGIE: I've felt like that too since my sister moved away. Usually it's in the middle of the night when I can't sleep. I just lay there and feel so alone. And think about how I should do it.

SARA: I know what you mean.

MAGGIE: Really?

SARA: I get home when they're all asleep. The whole house is dark and quiet. It's so empty. I feel so empty.

MAGGIE: God, I just wish—

SARA: What?

MAGGIE: The next time I'm feeling lousy, could I call you?

SARA: If I'm home.

MAGGIE: Or if you're feeling lousy you can call me—or come over. Even if it's like three in the morning.

SARA: Look. Just forget about it, okay?

(Pause.)

MAGGIE: Okay.

(Pause. MAGGIE and SARA leave the washroom area.)

Hey listen, by the way ...

SARA: Yeah?

MAGGIE: There's something I'm supposed to ask you.

SARA: What?

MAGGIE: You know Bob?

SARA: Bob?

MAGGIE: You know, Bob. Bob Bob.

SARA: Oh yeah, that Bob. He's sweet.

MAGGIE: Yeah.

SARA: He's nice.

MAGGIE: He likes you.

SARA: ... You don't mean like ...?

MAGGIE: Yeah, I mean like ...

SARA: Ohh.

MAGGIE: What do you think?

SARA: We're just friends. You know what I mean?

(LUKE enters.)

LUKE: Hi, baby.

SARA: Luke.

(SARA runs to him, they kiss.)

LUKE: What were you doing?

SARA: Nothing much.

LUKE: You weren't by your locker.

SARA: I was just having a smoke.

LUKE: You said you were gonna meet me there.

SARA: You're early.

LUKE: I'm early?

SARA: Aren't you?

LUKE: I've been waiting for fifteen minutes.

SARA: I was in the washroom.

LUKE: You should tell me these things.

SARA: I know.

LUKE: How am I supposed to know what you're doing?

SARA: I'm sorry, darlin'.

LUKE: Yeah?

(SARA kisses him.)

SARA: Yeah.

(Pause.)

LUKE: Now, the pants she's got on are nice. *(To MAGGIE.)* Have we met before?

SARA: This is Maggie.

LUKE: I know you. You're the student council rep.

MAGGIE: Yeah.

LUKE: You gave that speech last week. The one about how pollution's gonna kill us all before the end of the semester.

MAGGIE: End of the century.

LUKE: That's what I said. I loved that speech.

MAGGIE: Thanks.

LUKE: You know, your hair is the best. Sara, you ready?

SARA: Yeah.

LUKE: Then let's go. I've got a spare.

SARA: Okay.

LUKE: Goodbye, Maggie. See you around, eh?

MAGGIE: See ya.

> *(LUKE and SARA exit. MAGGIE watches them go, then leaves. From behind the screen, we see Luke's FATHER. LUKE enters.)*

FATHER: Lucas? I looked in my wallet this morning.

LUKE: So?

FATHER: Twenty dollars was missing, young man.

LUKE: I'm sorry to hear it.

FATHER: Do you know where it went?

LUKE: How should I know?

FATHER: Oh, I think you know.

LUKE: Well, I don't.

FATHER: Look into my eyes.

> *(LUKE faces the audience. Suddenly he is jerked back as if his FATHER has pulled his head back to look into his eyes.)*

Look! ... Very interesting. I can see everything, you can't hide a thing from me.

LUKE: I didn't take your money!

FATHER: I see a soul floating around in that darkness, Lucas. And it's dissolving into putrid stinking scum. You're a filthy liar, Lucas. I can see it in your tiny stupid eyes.

LUKE: I don't have it. I spent it!

FATHER: I want my money, young man. Tomorrow. Or it's your ass.

> (*FATHER exits. After a pause, LUKE gathers himself and struts off. BOB and MAGGIE enter, late for class. They smile at the teacher, sit down and start whispering.*)

BOB: So how did it go, how did it go?

MAGGIE: Fine, it went fine.

BOB: Yeah, so?

MAGGIE: Yeah so what?

BOB: So what did she say?

MAGGIE: A lot of things.

BOB: Like what?

MAGGIE: Things are really messed up for her, you know.

BOB: Yeah, so?

MAGGIE: It's not "yeah, so" Bob, it's bad!

> (*The teacher clears his throat. BOB and MAGGIE look up at the teacher, then dive back into their books. Slight pause. BOB starts whispering to MAGGIE again.*)

BOB: So what did she say about me?

MAGGIE: Wise up, Bob. God. I thought I had it rough. She can't even go home at night.

BOB: Why?

MAGGIE: All I know is it's bad.

BOB: Really terrible, huh?

MAGGIE: That's what I'm trying to tell you. It's awful. And that Luke—he's weird.

BOB: He is? Great!

MAGGIE: No it's not, there's something wrong there. That guy is paranoid!

TEACHER: (*Off.*) Shh!!

> (*BOB and MAGGIE look up at the teacher, then down at their books. Slight pause and BOB is whispering to her again.*)

BOB: See? She shouldn't be with him. She needs a different kind of guy. Somebody who's supportive. And sensitive. And decent.

MAGGIE: You're not kidding.

BOB: So what did she say?

MAGGIE: I don't believe what a goof you are.

BOB: I am?

MAGGIE: I don't believe what a goof I am to even be talking to a goof like you.

BOB: That's 'cause you're desperate for my companionship.

MAGGIE: Well, it's a disgusting condition and it makes me puke!

TEACHER: *(Off.)* Margaret!

MAGGIE: *(Innocently.)* Yes, sir?

TEACHER: *(Off.)* Robert!

BOB: Sir?

TEACHER: You're outta here.

BOB and MAGGIE: But sir, he—she—

> *(They point at each other.)*

TEACHER: Out!

> *(They both pick up their books and leave class. As soon as they leave the class area, MAGGIE hits BOB with a book.)*

MAGGIE: Thanks a lot, Bob!

BOB: What did she say about me?

MAGGIE: She thinks you're sweet.

BOB: Me? Sweet? She thinks I'm sweet! I can't believe it! Sweet! I'm sweet! She thinks I'm sweet! ... What else did she say?

MAGGIE: She said you were nice.

BOB: Nice. Nice. Well, it's sort of like love.

MAGGIE: What?

BOB: They're both four-letter words. Nice. Nice. What does nice mean? Like, what's the deeper meaning? Dictionary.

> *(BOB gets out a dictionary.)*

Let's see: 1. Very careful. Refined. Hmm. 2. Delicate, subtle ... that's me, for sure.

MAGGIE: For sure.

BOB: 3. Having high standards of conduct.

MAGGIE: That's you, absolutely.

BOB: Think so? 4. Agreeable. Pleasant. Delightful. Alllright!! 5. Kind, thoughtful, considerate. I'm on a roll! Ignorant, stupid, foolish ... what? ... Oh my God. I thought nice was good. She thinks I'm ignorant, stupid and foolish!

MAGGIE: She's a smart girl.

BOB: I don't believe it. Nice. Oh no. I might as well be dead.

MAGGIE: Look at this thing, dope. Just before that definition it says O-B-S.

BOB: O-b-s? Obs? What's Obs?

MAGGIE: It means obsolete. The word nice isn't used that way anymore. It's like record albums.

BOB: I knew that. But how do I know she didn't mean it that way? She thinks I'm nice as in obs nice.

MAGGIE: She thinks of you as a friend.

BOB: Did she say that?

MAGGIE: Yes.

BOB: Then there is hope. Nice as in delightful. Agreeable. Pleasant. She thinks I'm delightful!

MAGGIE: Bob, will you snap out of it? Look at her as a person. She needs help!

BOB: I look at her as a person. I see her completely. I'm not blind.

MAGGIE: Wake up, Bob.

> *(MAGGIE exits.)*

BOB: I am up, Maggie. I am. Maggie? *(To audience.)* Maybe I do get carried away. But love is like that. It makes you a little crazy. You can't be responsible for everything you do.

> *(BOB's parents behind screen.)*

DAD: Bobby! Do you know what happened to the TV guide?

BOB: Don't tell me—it ran off with a *People* magazine.

MOM: I knew it, he's not studying, he's squeezing pepperoni out of his nose.

> *(BOB snorts.)*

DAD: Bobby! Are you catching a cold, son?

BOB: No, Dad.

DAD: Well, take some Anacin. Take some Neo Citran. Take some 222s.

MOM: You sound just like a commercial!

DAD: If he's sick, he needs the best.

MOM: What he needs is a kick in the ass.

BOB: Oh Lord! It's a miracle! I'm healed!

DAD: How am I supposed to watch TV without a TV guide?

BOB: I got faith, you can do it, Dad.

MOM: Why do I care? Go ahead, be a waste like your father.

BOB: What?

MOM: You're a waste!

BOB: *(Quietly.)* Thanks, Mom.

MOM: *(Loudly.)* You're welcome!

  (Parents exit. SARA enters, wearing sun-glasses.)

BOB: I like your shades.

SARA: Thanks.

BOB: They're great, where'd you get them?

SARA: They were a gift.

BOB: Can I try them on?

SARA: Why?

BOB: I think they're nice.

SARA: They're not that nice.

BOB: Sure they are, they're hot.

SARA: They're nothing special.

BOB: Sure they are, they're great, come on!

  (BOB takes them off SARA. She has a black eye. Pause.)
  God, your eye. What happened?

SARA: I fell.

BOB: You fell? How'd you fall?

SARA: I fell, alright!

BOB: Sorry.

SARA: ... Luke hit me.

BOB: He did? Why?

SARA: Sometimes he gets mad, that's all.

BOB: He's done it before?

SARA: Oh yeah.

BOB: Why?

SARA: ... I was late.

(*LUKE enters. SARA runs to him.*)

LUKE: You know what time it is?

SARA: No, no, am I late?

LUKE: We said eight sharp. It's eight-thirty!

SARA: I'm sorry, Luke.

LUKE: Sorry? Sorry! What were you doing?

SARA: I was cleaning up, I lost track of—

LUKE: Don't tell me your stupid stinking lies!

SARA: Luke!

LUKE: You're a filthy liar!

(*LUKE backhands her across the face. She goes down. Beat.*)
Sara? Sara? Are you okay? Sara? Sara, please, be okay. Sara, I'm sorry. Sara.

SARA: (*Coming to.*) Luke?

LUKE: I'm sorry, baby, I'm so sorry.

SARA: I'm okay.

LUKE: Thank God. I'm sorry, darling, I'm out of my mind.

SARA: No you're not.

LUKE: I don't know why I lose it, I'm so crazy.

SARA: Please don't do it again.

LUKE: I won't, I swear it, that was the last time. You think I want to risk losing you? If I lost you, I'd die, you know. I'll kill myself.

SARA: Don't talk like that.

LUKE: Believe me, I would. What else would I live for? I'd take my dad's gun and blow my brains out.

SARA: Don't, Luke, stop it.

LUKE: Without you I'm nothing. You're the only person in the world who understands me. If you leave me I'm a dead man.

SARA: I won't leave you, I promise, I won't leave you.

> *(LUKE exits.)*

BOB: What are you doing with that guy, he's crazy.

SARA: So am I.

BOB: No you're not, there's nothing wrong with you.

> *(In the background, the voices of MARY and JOE.)*

JOE: You stink, you know that? Why don't you ever wash?

SARA: He's the only person crazy enough to understand me.

MARY: I need you so much, Joe.

BOB: But nobody has the right to hit another person.

SARA: People do it all the time.

JOE: If I ever catch you with him, I'll kill you.

BOB: That doesn't make it right.

MARY: Joe, stop it!

> *(JOE and MARY vanish from screen. We hear the sound of JOE hitting MARY.)*

BOB: It's against the law. How can you let somebody do that to you?

SARA: Oh, come on, it's no big deal.

BOB: Yes it is. How can you take it?

SARA: I just do.

BOB: But he hits you.

SARA: Only if something pisses him off.

BOB: He's crazy, Sara.

SARA: You don't know what you're talking about. You don't know him at all.

BOB: I know enough.

SARA: No. You don't understand. I love him.

BOB: ... You're right. I don't understand.

> *(BOB exits.)*

SARA: You don't know what he's been through. It's not his fault the way he's been screwed around since he was a little kid.

> *(Luke's FATHER enters behind screen.)*

FATHER: Lucas.

(LUKE, as a child, enters. He is carrying a toy football and wears a T-shirt that evokes youth. The shirt (or other costume/ prop) should not be comic. A simple yellow shirt with perhaps a team number would be enough.)

LUKE: Yes, Dad?

FATHER: I thought you had three hamsters, young man.

LUKE: I do.

FATHER: All I see here are two.

LUKE: Only two?

FATHER: I bought you three hamsters for that cage. One of them is missing. Where's the third hamster?

LUKE: I don't know.

FATHER: You don't know? One of your hamsters is missing and you don't know?

LUKE: No.

FATHER: Toes and fingers.

LUKE: No.

FATHER: Toes and fingers!

(LUKE stands on tiptoes, hands high over head.)

What happened to it? What happened?

LUKE: I don't know.

FATHER: I think you do.

(FATHER swings arm. Slapping sound. LUKE's face jerks right.)

Now, talk!

(Luke's MOTHER enters.)

MOTHER: What are you doing to him?

LUKE: Mom!

FATHER: Get out of here!

MOTHER: Don't hurt him.

LUKE: Mom!

FATHER: Get out!

(FATHER shoves MOTHER off.)

(To LUKE.) Talk!

LUKE: I took them outside. One got away.

FATHER: You lost it? You lost a hamster? Do you realize what you've done?

LUKE: I'm sorry.

FATHER: Sorry? It hasn't got a chance out there. You might as well have crushed its head!

(*FATHER swings. Slapping sound. LUKE's face jerks.*)

Don't cry, be a man. You killed it!

(*He hits LUKE again.*)

You killed that poor little thing!

(*He hits LUKE once more and exits.*)

SARA: It was just a stupid hamster.

(*Music. In this short sequence we see the child LUKE transform into the teen LUKE. The child sits in a huddled position, rocking himself. He stops, throwing the toy football away. Gradually he stands, tearing off the T-shirt of his childhood, filled with rage. LUKE goes to SARA.*)

LUKE: What were you talking to that guy for?

SARA: We were just talking.

LUKE: You know I don't like it when you talk to other guys.

SARA: It was nothing, really.

LUKE: How am I supposed to know that?

SARA: 'Cause I told you.

LUKE: I can't watch you every second, I can't keep you on a leash.

SARA: I wouldn't want you to.

LUKE: How do I know you're not cheating on me?

SARA: 'Cause I'm not.

LUKE: Then why are you wearing your hair like that?

SARA: I just put some clips in it. Don't you like it?

LUKE: It makes you look like a slut.

SARA: Everybody wears these things.

LUKE: You're not everybody. You're with me. Only whores dress like that.

SARA: I'll take them out.

LUKE: I like your hair normal. So you wear it just for me.

SARA: No problem.

LUKE: Who was that guy?

SARA: You know him, Bob.

LUKE: You in love with him or something?

SARA: No way.

LUKE: I saw the way you looked at him.

SARA: Luke, he's just a friend, I don't care about him like that. Not like I care about you.

LUKE: Then I don't want to see you talking to him.

SARA: Okay. No problem.

LUKE: I don't want you looking at him.

SARA: I won't. Don't worry. Okay?

LUKE: Okay. Let's go.

SARA: Okay.

    (They exit. MAGGIE and BOB enter, watching them exit.)

BOB: I'd like to just kill that guy, I'd like to just rip his heart out.

MAGGIE: That'd be a big help, Bob.

BOB: I cannot understand how she can stay with that maniac. You shoulda seen her eye!

MAGGIE: I saw it.

BOB: Why would she want to be with somebody like that? He hurts her! Do you think she likes to be hurt?

MAGGIE: I sincerely doubt that, Bob.

BOB: It doesn't make any sense to me, I cannot figure it out. God, I'm starving. What do you have for lunch today?

MAGGIE: Tuna fish.

    (BOB takes MAGGIE's lunch bag and starts looking through it.)

BOB: Smarties! A little box of Smarties! Were you out trick or treating on Hallowe'en? What were you dressed as? Little Red Riding Hood?

MAGGIE: They were leftovers.

BOB: Sure. I believe you. Oh, great, here it is.

    (He pulls out a small sandwich.)

What's this? You call this a sandwich? Trying to shed a few extra pounds, Maggie? ... No onions in it, is there?

MAGGIE: No.

(BOB eats.)

BOB: I mean, how can a guy get off treating a girl like that? Who does he think he is?

MAGGIE: He thinks he's superior to her.

BOB: Obviously. God, Maggie, anybody could have figured that out. Mind if I drink your juice?

MAGGIE: What difference does it make?

BOB: It makes a big difference! He walks all over her. What gives him the right?

MAGGIE: Nothing.

BOB: Exactly! Just a sandwich and some juice? Is that all you had?

MAGGIE: I wasn't that hungry.

BOB: Well, I'm starved. I guess I'll have to eat the Smarties.

MAGGIE: I guess so.

BOB: If I get any zits, it'll be your fault.

MAGGIE: Of course.

BOB: Nobody should be able to do that to another person. Bullying her, taking advantage of her, doing whatever he wants. I'll tell you something, Maggie, seeing that black eye on Sara really changed my life.

(BOB crumples up the empty Smarties box and hands it and the empty bag and wrappers to MAGGIE.)

MAGGIE: Really?

BOB: Really.

MAGGIE: I'm glad to hear it.

(MAGGIE takes all the papers and shoves them down BOB's back.)

BOB: What did you do that for?

MAGGIE: Think about it.

BOB: You're mad. You're mad about something ... What's the matter with you?

MAGGIE: Where's my lunch, jerk?

BOB: Oh. Sorry.

MAGGIE: And not only did you stuff your face with it, but you were putting me down the whole time! "God, Maggie, anybody could have figured that out!" "Trying to shed a few extra pounds, Maggie?"

BOB: I didn't mean it like that.

MAGGIE: How else could you have meant it?

BOB: I don't know.

MAGGIE: So how come you treat me like that? What gives you the right?

(*We hear the voices of Bob's parents.*)

DAD: Don't badger the boy.

BOB: Why're you badgering me?

MAGGIE: 'Cause it really burns me when you do that!

MOM: What he needs is a kick in the ass.

MAGGIE: You think Luke's bad, look at yourself!

MOM: What are you doing with your life?

MAGGIE: This is important, Bob, you haveta look at it!

DAD: Oop, halftime's over, gotta go!

BOB: Oop, gotta go—

MAGGIE: You really are the same as Luke.

BOB: Quit saying that to me!

MAGGIE: Well, you will be if you don't do something!

MOM: What do I care? Go ahead, be a waste like your father.

DAD: Leave the boy alone.

BOB: Will you just leave me alone!

MAGGIE: Don't you think I deserve to be upset? Don't you want to change?

DAD: No.

MOM: No.

BOB: No.

MAGGIE: Thanks a lot, Bob.

BOB and MOM: You're welcome!

(*BOB exits.*)

MAGGIE: Bob, get back here! Bob!

   (End of Act One.)

Act Two

(Morning. We see the four kids in silhouette, waking up in their respective beds. Lights up on BOB.)

BOB: I am dabbing my face with cover-up stick. Forget it, Bob. This is not something that you can hide. Your whole idiot face is an open book.

(Lights on MAGGIE, practising her martial arts.)

God, she pisses me off. "Change, Bob, change!" Well, why should I? What's wrong with the way I am?

(Slight pause while BOB thinks about that one.)

Okay, so I should change. But I'm not the same as Luke, she's full of it.

(Lights on LUKE, combing his hair. This is a precise and exacting ritual.)

Teasing somebody about their weight isn't the same as being a demented sadist.

(BOB and LUKE look closely at their hair. Both pull out a few stray hairs at the same time.)

But I guess we do have one thing in common ...

(Lights on SARA, who lights a cigarette.)

... we're both in love with her—though why she's with him is a mystery to me.

(SARA examines a new bruise on her arm. LUKE turns and goes.)

It's easy for Maggie to talk, her life's so perfect.

(MAGGIE finishes her exercises and faces herself in the mirror. She isn't very happy.)

Oh, cheer up, Bob, one day your life'll be perfect too. Ha.

(BOB and MAGGIE start to go at the same time. They see each other. Slight pause. Exit in different directions.

Lights intensify on SARA who holds out her arm, about to burn herself with the cigarette. Pause. She decides against it, drops the cigarette on the ground and crushes it with her foot. She looks up, blowing smoke in the air.

BOB enters the boys' workout room and starts to bench-press a weight. It pins him down.)

BOB: Uh ... help!

(LUKE, out of BOB's view, sizes him up, then goes to him.)

LUKE: Hey, Mr. Bob!

BOB: Luke.

LUKE: How're ya doin?

BOB: Pretty good.

LUKE: You workin out?

BOB: Yeah, thought maybe, sort of.

(LUKE puts the weight back on the bar, freeing BOB.)

LUKE: You got a program or something?

BOB: Me? Sure, I walk a lot.

LUKE: Why don't you let me show you some stuff?

BOB: That's okay.

LUKE: Ah, come on. You got all the stuff it takes to ...

BOB: Pump iron?

LUKE: Well, sure, why not—you got good tone and everything. A little work, you'd be there.

BOB: You're kidding.

LUKE: No way. Try some of these push-ups.

(LUKE quickly does a half dozen clapping push-ups.)

BOB: You want me to do that?

LUKE: Go on, they're easy. A kid could do 'em. They're great for the pecs.

BOB: Great for the pecs, huh?

(BOB gets into the position. He pushes up, tries to clap, falls on his face.)

LUKE: That's good, that's great.

BOB: I practically killed myself.

LUKE: You just about had it. Try again.

BOB: I don't know.

LUKE: Do it.

(BOB tries again, fails.)

Excellent attempt. Do it again.

BOB: Maybe I should try something else.

(LUKE helps BOB up.)

LUKE: How 'bout your stomach?

(LUKE makes a move to punch BOB in his stomach.)

Hey, man, you gotta be ready for anything.

BOB: Yeah.

LUKE: I'll show you a good way to do sit-ups.

BOB: I don't know.

LUKE: This method, you do every day, in two weeks you could take a punch from Hulk Hogan.

BOB: Do I have to?

LUKE: Get down, I'll hold your feet.

(BOB does.)

Keep your knees up. Good, go ahead.

(BOB starts doing sit-ups.)

Great, nice and slow. You just work out an hour a day, you can take anything. Your whole body gets like metal, nothing touches you. You sit near Sara in English?

BOB: Well, same room.

LUKE: I saw you sitting next to her.

BOB: Well, yeah, I have.

LUKE: She any good?

BOB: Sure, I don't know.

LUKE: You don't know?

BOB: I don't check out her grades.

LUKE: You don't?

BOB: No.

> *(LUKE suddenly lets go of BOB's legs and makes like he's going for his face.)*

What are you doing!

LUKE: You gotta be on your toes, man, or you'll get blind-sided.

BOB: Right.

> *(BOB stops.)*

LUKE: Keep going.

BOB: How much longer?

LUKE: I'll tell you when.

BOB: I'm getting kinda sore.

LUKE: Good, then you know you're getting results.

BOB: Really?

LUKE: Absolutely. What do you talk to Sara about?

BOB: School, you know, the usual.

LUKE: The usual.

BOB: She's nice.

LUKE: Yeah, she's really nice. Faster!

BOB: Faster?

LUKE: Yeah, fast. Go!

> *(BOB does.)*

Don't stop, keep going, don't quit!

BOB: I can't—

LUKE: You will!

BOB: I'm dying—

LUKE: More!

> *(BOB collapses. LUKE smiles.)*

That was great, Bob. Really great. You're in way better shape than you thought.

BOB: I am?

LUKE: You'll be a little stiff tomorrow but don't let that stop you working out. Best time is when it hurts. That Maggie is quite the catch. How long you two been an item?

BOB: Me and Maggie?

LUKE: Yeah, the way you two hang out you'd think you were clamped together.

BOB: Really?

LUKE: She's quite the find, man.

BOB: You really think so?

LUKE: It's a great set-up, to be with somebody like that.

BOB: Yeah, I guess so.

LUKE: I bet she's wild.

BOB: She can be, yeah.

LUKE: That's good, nothing's worse than a cold fish.

BOB: Nothing.

LUKE: You're a lucky man, Mr. Bob.

BOB: You're pretty lucky yourself.

LUKE: *(Suddenly cool.)* I am?

BOB: I mean, going out with Sara.

LUKE: She's going out with me.

BOB: Right. That's what I meant.

LUKE: Good.

>   *(LUKE turns warm again.)*

You just keep doing those sit-ups and you'll be a tough man to beat.

BOB: Okay.

>   *(LUKE fakes a punch to BOB's face. BOB lurches.)*

LUKE: Good reflexes. Very good.

>   *(LUKE exits, BOB watches him go. Lights on MAGGIE in the washroom, pushing her cheeks up so it looks like she has cheekbones. SARA furtively enters.)*

MAGGIE: Hi.

SARA: Hi.

>   *(SARA woozy, leans over.)*

MAGGIE: Are you okay?

SARA: Yeah.

MAGGIE: You sure? Want some water or something?

SARA: It's nothing, musta ate breakfast too fast.

MAGGIE: You look kinda out of it. Let me wet a paper towel for your face.

SARA: I'll be okay, thanks.

(SARA looks in the mirror.)

God, I look like hell.

MAGGIE: When you look bad, you still look great. I sure wish I had cheekbones.

SARA: What're you talking about?

MAGGIE: Chipmunk cheeks. And thunder thighs. You could slice slabs off them with a knife.

SARA: You're not fat.

MAGGIE: I'm not you. Hey, your hands are shaking.

SARA: I had a rough morning. Tryin' to get that math homework done.

MAGGIE: You should've phoned me, I could've helped.

SARA: Maybe it's the flu or something.

MAGGIE: I wonder if I put the lighter stuff here people could see my eyes.

SARA: You got great eyes.

MAGGIE: My cheeks hide them. You sure you're okay?

SARA: I have a weak stomach.

MAGGIE: My mom too. Things get to her easy.

SARA: Nerves?

MAGGIE: She's a real mess.

SARA: Aren't all moms screwed up?

MAGGIE: No, I've seen a couple in my life that were real nice.

SARA: We had another fight.

MAGGIE: Oh no. Did he—

SARA: Just my arm.

(MAGGIE looks.)

MAGGIE: Oh God, Sara, you gotta dump that guy.

SARA: You don't know him.

MAGGIE: I know enough. He's hurting you.

SARA: He just loses it sometimes.

MAGGIE: You're not kidding.

SARA: It only happens 'cause of me, I make him do it.

MAGGIE: How can you make somebody do that?

SARA: Tons of ways, little ways, I do it all the time.

MAGGIE: You mean like being late, or wearing the wrong pants or talking to the wrong person?

   (SARA is silent.)

Come on, Sara, there's nothing wrong with that, he's just bullying you.

SARA: If I left he'd kill himself, or he'd kill me.

MAGGIE: He's just threatening you.

SARA: He wouldn't leave me alone. I couldn't fight him.

MAGGIE: We could get you help.

SARA: You don't know Luke.

MAGGIE: You want to be his prisoner for the rest of your life?

SARA: ... No.

MAGGIE: Then you gotta break up with him.

   (LUKE's shadow appears outside the washroom door.)

LUKE: Sara, you in there? Sara?

   (SARA frantically grabs MAGGIE. Pause.)

Sara? Sara answer me!

   (The girls hold each other. Pause.)

SARA: *(Weakly.)* Yeah, Luke?

LUKE: What are you doing?

SARA: I'll be out in a minute.

MAGGIE: You don't have to go out there if you don't want to.

LUKE: What's goin' on?

SARA: I'm just on the can.

LUKE: So hurry up.

SARA: I will, Luke, I will.

LUKE: I'll meet you outside.

> *(LUKE goes. SARA listens to hear that he's gone, then runs to MAGGIE.)*

SARA: Maggie, you gotta help me, please.

MAGGIE: Sure, Sara.

SARA: Tell him I'm sick, tell him I'm going to the nurse, tell him something.

MAGGIE: Sure, I'll do it, don't worry.

SARA: I just can't face him right now.

MAGGIE: I know.

SARA: I couldn't talk to him.

MAGGIE: It's okay.

SARA: But I'm gonna. I'm gonna tell him. I can't take it anymore, Maggie.

MAGGIE: It's okay, it's okay, I'll talk to him, don't worry. You gonna be alright?

SARA: Uh huh. Thanks.

> *(MAGGIE exits. The lights fade on SARA as she lights a cigarette. LUKE is standing, waiting for SARA. MAGGIE approaches him.)*

MAGGIE: Luke.

LUKE: How're you doin', Maggie?

MAGGIE: Sara told me to give you a message—she's got some kind of bug.

LUKE: You were in the washroom?

MAGGIE: Yeah, she was puking her guts out.

LUKE: Oh God, is she gonna be okay?

MAGGIE: Oh, yeah, I'm sure.

LUKE: I should go help her—

MAGGIE: You don't have to worry, really. As soon as she's up to it, she's going to see the nurse.

LUKE: That sounds bad.

MAGGIE: She'll be fine. She said she'll catch up with you later.

LUKE: You sure?

MAGGIE: Oh, yeah.

LUKE: Well, thanks for telling me, Maggie.

MAGGIE: No problem.

LUKE: ... It's no bug.

MAGGIE: What?

LUKE: It's me.

MAGGIE: What are you talking about?

LUKE: I upset her. I keep upsetting her.

MAGGIE: You think so?

LUKE: Can I talk to you?

MAGGIE: Sure, of course you can.

LUKE: I got nobody to talk to about this.

MAGGIE: About what?

LUKE: Sara and me. I'm losing her.

MAGGIE: What makes you say that?

LUKE: I know it, I can tell.

MAGGIE: Is it something she's doing?

LUKE: It's what I'm doing. I push her away from me. I'm making her hate me.

MAGGIE: Why?

LUKE: I love her so much, Maggie. I love her more than my whole life. I get jealous.

MAGGIE: You don't have to.

LUKE: It just goes right through my blood, streams into my brain, I go blind.

MAGGIE: You gotta fight it.

LUKE: I try.

MAGGIE: You gotta try harder. Or you could lose her.

LUKE: You really think I could?

MAGGIE: Yeah.

LUKE: I'm not gonna lose her, Maggie. I'll do anything to be with her.

MAGGIE: Then change.

LUKE: I want to, it's just knowing how.

MAGGIE: Maybe you need help.

LUKE: Sometimes I get so confused, I don't know where to go.

MAGGIE: I know what you mean.

LUKE: You do, don't you?

MAGGIE: Um hm.

LUKE: Thank you, Maggie.

>   *(LUKE gives MAGGIE's face a gentle stroke.)*

I can really talk to you. I usually feel so alone—but we can talk. Do you and Bob talk like this?

MAGGIE: Yeah, once every year or so.

LUKE: He doesn't know what he has.

MAGGIE: I guess not.

LUKE: How long have you been together?

MAGGIE: I'm not sure I get your drift.

LUKE: Yes you do.

MAGGIE: Together? Like boyfriend/girlfriend? As in "my main squeeze"?

LUKE: Right.

MAGGIE: No. We're just friends.

LUKE: Well, he gets around.

MAGGIE: Bob?

LUKE: Yeah, Bob.

MAGGIE: You mean the Bob I hang out with?

LUKE: Yeah, that Bob.

MAGGIE: You must be thinking of a different Bob.

LUKE: No, I mean that Bob.

MAGGIE: That Bob?

LUKE: That Bob.

MAGGIE: You learn something new every day.

LUKE: I figured you two were together 'cause of what I heard you did.

MAGGIE: What did we do?

LUKE: You know.

MAGGIE: I haven't a clue.

LUKE: You don't have to pretend with me.

MAGGIE: I'm not pretending.

LUKE: Everybody knows about it.

MAGGIE: Knows about what?

LUKE: About you and Bob in the—

MAGGIE: Me and Bob in the what?

LUKE: In the washroom.

MAGGIE: In the washroom? What were we doing in the washroom?

LUKE: You know.

MAGGIE: That? Me and Bob? Doing that in the washroom?

    (She laughs.)

  Which one did we do it in? The boys' or girls'? Staff? On a toilet or in it?

LUKE: I don't know but I thought it was pretty cool, doing something like that.

    (LUKE touches MAGGIE, she pulls away.)

MAGGIE: Cut it out.

LUKE: You didn't stop me before, why now?

MAGGIE: 'Cause before—before was different.

LUKE: Were you teasing me?

MAGGIE: No. I mean—

LUKE: So why spoil something nice?

MAGGIE: You're the one who's spoiling it.

LUKE: You don't have to worry about Bob. He'll never have to know.

MAGGIE: What about Sara?

LUKE: What about her?

MAGGIE: What would she think about all this?

LUKE: It's our secret.

MAGGIE: Look, Luke, I'm not interested.

LUKE: Sure you are.

MAGGIE: No I'm not.

LUKE: I know how to make you interested.

>*(LUKE embraces her.)*

MAGGIE: Let go of me!

LUKE: Bob said you were wild.

>*(MAGGIE breaks away.)*

MAGGIE: He what?

LUKE: He said you did it all the time.

MAGGIE: That creep!

LUKE: Don't worry about him, it's just us now.

>*(He goes for her again.)*

MAGGIE: Back off, Luke.

>*(LUKE embraces her.)*

LUKE: Don't fight it, feel it.

MAGGIE: Cut it out!

LUKE: I know you want it.

MAGGIE: No!

LUKE: Come on …

MAGGIE: No!

>*(And MAGGIE, using a self-defence move, elbows LUKE in the solar plexus. He falls to his knees.)*

I said no, I meant no!

LUKE: Hey, what's the matter, we were just talking.

MAGGIE: You wouldn't back off, Luke.

LUKE: I wasn't doing anything.

MAGGIE: You assaulted me.

LUKE: Who assaulted who?

MAGGIE: Alright, that's it, I'm going to the office to call the cops.

LUKE: No, no, okay, okay, I'm sorry. I'm really sorry.

MAGGIE: If you ever try anything like that again …

LUKE: I won't, really, I was wrong. You were just being so nice, I thought I saw something in your eyes. I did.

MAGGIE: If somebody says no, you listen!

LUKE: Okay, okay. I promise.

(Pause.)

It never happened.

(LUKE goes. MAGGIE watches him go, then sits. BOB enters.)

BOB: Howya doin?

MAGGIE: Fine.

BOB: I'm sorry about before. About blowing up. You were right. I should change. I'm gonna try.

MAGGIE: Forget it.

BOB: You're still mad at me.

MAGGIE: Just leave me alone, will you? Just go.

BOB: I said I was sorry.

MAGGIE: I don't want to talk to you, you're a creep. I don't know how you could do that.

BOB: Maggie, I swear, I'll never eat your lunch again.

MAGGIE: You jerk! How long have we been friends? How can you stand there and look at me—after saying that—

BOB: Saying what?

MAGGIE: You were always there, you might be a goof but you never let me down.

BOB: What did I say?

MAGGIE: And behind my back—how could you? In the washroom.

BOB: The what?

MAGGIE: Don't deny it! He said I did it with you, now I can do it with the whole damn school!

BOB: Who said?

MAGGIE: Luke said!

BOB: But Maggie, I—

MAGGIE: And then he grabbed me 'cause you said it, 'cause you said that about me!

BOB: Maggie, listen to me—

MAGGIE: Don't you touch me!

(Short pause. SARA enters.)

SARA: Are you okay?

MAGGIE: Yeah, I'm fine.

SARA: Thanks for helping me out.

MAGGIE: Forget it.

SARA: Did he say anything?

MAGGIE: Everything's fine. I gotta go.

>   *(MAGGIE goes.)*

SARA: Maggie? What happened?

BOB: Luke grabbed her.

>   *(Pause.)*

SARA: What was she doing?

BOB: What do you mean?

SARA: She must've been doing something.

BOB: Like what?

SARA: Girls are always throwing themselves at him.

BOB: That doesn't sound like Maggie.

SARA: She must have been asking for it.

BOB: Yeah, Maggie's a real nymphomaniac.

SARA: Well, he wouldn't force himself on her unless she did something, unless she made him do it.

BOB: How can you make somebody do that?

SARA: There are tons of ways.

BOB: No, Sara, you can't.

SARA: Look, you don't know a thing about what's going on, not a damn thing, so why don't you just keep your nose out of it!

BOB: Okay.

>   *(SARA goes. BOB watches her, then exits, miserable. MAGGIE enters, and her MOTHER appears behind screen, drinking.)*

MOTHER: Thank God you're home, Maggie.

MAGGIE: Why, what is it?

MOTHER: I've been missing you.

MAGGIE: I've been missing you too.

MOTHER: I feel so trapped, Maggie.

MAGGIE: Me too.

MOTHER: He must hate me.

MAGGIE: Dad doesn't hate you, Mom.

MOTHER: He never comes home. He's probably in bed right now with some twenty-year-old.

MAGGIE: He wouldn't do that to you.

MOTHER: I don't blame him. I look like an old lady. My whole body is sagging into the ground.

MAGGIE: No it's not, Mom.

MOTHER: You're my best friend, aren't you? The only person in the whole world I can count on.

MAGGIE: You'll be okay, Mom.

MOTHER: If I didn't have you to be close to me, I don't know what I'd do.

MAGGIE: I've had a really rough day, Mom.

MOTHER: I'm so tired.

> *(MOTHER fades out.)*

MAGGIE: It's kind of hard to talk about, you know?

> *(MAGGIE realizes she's passed out.)*

I guess I'll be in my room.

> *(MAGGIE exits. LUKE approaches SARA.)*

LUKE: Baby, are you feeling better?

SARA: Yeah.

LUKE: I was worried about you.

SARA: What do you care?

LUKE: What's wrong, what is it?

SARA: I heard what happened with Maggie.

LUKE: What about it?

SARA: I know what you tried to do, Luke.

LUKE: Sara, listen to me, it's not what you think.

SARA: Then what is it?

LUKE: She was all over me, there was nothing I could do.

SARA: Bull!

LUKE: Nothing happened, I swear it!

SARA: ... How can I stay with you when you do these things?

LUKE: Don't talk like that.

SARA: How could you do it?

LUKE: Don't say that about leaving. Never say that.

SARA: What else can I say?

LUKE: Just never say that to me. Don't even think it!

SARA: Then why do you do these things?

LUKE: I don't mean it to happen, it just happens. We were talking, she was being nice, I started thinking about her and that Bob guy and how he looks at you.

SARA: Most people just think it. You go and do it.

LUKE: I can't help it. I can't help what's in my brain and what it makes me do, Sara. All I know is I love you. I'm nothing without you. You gotta forgive me.

SARA: All I ever do is forgive you.

LUKE: Without you I'd just fry up, I'd just crash and burn.

SARA: Don't talk like that.

LUKE: Tell me you love me.

SARA: ... I love you.

LUKE: Sara, remember: We loved each other a thousand years ago. But we were caught and they chained our bodies together and threw us into the sea. We sank through the water with our lips still together, a kiss that never ended. It's our souls that just met again, in this life. It took a thousand years but we found each other. And now we can never be apart again. Never.

SARA: ... Never.

   (Lights on BOB, dialing the phone.)

BOB: If her stupid mom answers it I'm gonna go crazy.

   (It rings, MAGGIE picks it up.)

MAGGIE: Hello?

BOB: Maggie, it's me, you gotta let me expl—

   (MAGGIE listens to him, thinks, then hangs up.)

   Maggie? Maggie?

   (He dials again.)

BOB: I may be a loser but I'm no quitter.

   (It rings. MAGGIE lets it ring a few times, then picks it up.)

MAGGIE: Hello?

BOB: *(Very fast.)* Maggie, you gotta listen to me, I'm really sorry— *(She hangs up.)* Somehow I don't think she wants to talk to me.

MOM: Bobby, who are you talking to?

BOB: The Pope!

DAD: Bob Hope?

MOM: No wonder he's flunking, all he does is yak on the phone. Yak, yak, yak.

DAD: Leave the boy alone.

MOM: We left him alone, look what happened!

BOB: Why don't you both just shut up and go away!

    (Pause.)

MOM: Did you hear what he said?

DAD: No, did you?

MOM: Bobby, what did you say?

BOB: You're driving me nuts!

    (Pause.)

DAD: See, you drive him crazy.

MOM: He didn't say I drove him crazy, he said you drove him crazy.

DAD: I heard what he said, he said you drove him crazy ...

    (BOB slams the door. He listens. It's quiet. He smiles for a moment, then dials the phone again. MAGGIE just watches the phone and lets it ring.)

BOB: Maggie, come on, please ... I really screwed it up this time. Maggie!

    (BOB hangs up, grabs his jacket and exits. MAGGIE, still sitting by the phone, hears a tapping sound. She goes to the window, opens it. It is SARA.)

MAGGIE: Come on in.

SARA: It's not too late?

MAGGIE: I told you anytime.

SARA: I woulda knocked on the door but I saw your mom asleep on the couch.

MAGGIE: Yeah, she's not doing so hot.

SARA: She had a bottle next to her.

MAGGIE: She'll get over it.

SARA: I know that story. Things are bad, huh?

MAGGIE: She just gets depressed when my dad's away.

SARA: How 'bout you?

MAGGIE: I'm fine.

SARA: You don't look fine.

MAGGIE: I am okay.

> *(Pause.)*

SARA: What happened today, Maggie?

> *(MAGGIE is silent.)*

Why won't you tell me what's going on?

> *(Pause.)*

MAGGIE: You asked me to talk to him, so I did.

SARA: Then what?

MAGGIE: He was worried about you and him—he wanted to talk about it, wanted my advice. It was okay at first but it got weird, he started saying things.

SARA: What kind of things?

MAGGIE: Things.... And then he was on me, grabbing me.

SARA: Luke.

MAGGIE: Yeah, Luke.... So how is his solar plexus?

SARA: His what?

MAGGIE: I caught him with a Hiji.

> *(MAGGIE demonstrates.)*

My Wen-Do instructor was right, it really works.

SARA: ... When I first heard I wasn't on your side. I thought you did something to make him come on to you. I figured you were trying to get between Luke and me.

MAGGIE: Do you still think that?

SARA: No. Luke admitted everything. He was really torn up.

MAGGIE: He should be. If it ever happens again, I'm going straight to the police. You should too.

SARA: Maggie, I love him. What's between us goes really deep. If I leave him, he'll hurt himself.

MAGGIE: If that's love, I don't want it. I want to be in love so I can be happy.

SARA: We are happy—sometimes.

MAGGIE: You gotta think of yourself, Sara.

SARA: But he can be so gentle. He needs me so much.

MAGGIE: As long as you're not late, or wearing the wrong pants or talking to the wrong person.

SARA: He doesn't mean to do it. He needs my help.

MAGGIE: You can't help him if you can't help yourself.

SARA: What can I tell him?

MAGGIE: That you're helping him by leaving him.

SARA: I'm scared.

MAGGIE: He's a scary guy. But don't wait till he beats you up again, Sara.

SARA: ... You just elbowed him in the gut?

MAGGIE: Yeah. First time I ever tried it for real. He went right down on his knees.

SARA: On his knees?

MAGGIE: Like he was praying. Except he made a face like this:

(MAGGIE grimaces.)

SARA: ... You think I could do it?

MAGGIE: A Hiji? With a little practice—

SARA: No, break up with him.

MAGGIE: Sure you can. I know you can.

(Pause. BOB is outside the window.)

BOB: Maggie! Maggie! Maggie!

SARA: Aren't you gonna answer him?

MAGGIE: No, we're not on speaking terms.

SARA: Why? What did he do?

MAGGIE: He spread lies about me.

BOB: Maggie, I'm outside! It's cold!

SARA: It is cold out there.

MAGGIE: Let him get frostbite.

BOB: If you don't let me in, I'll wake up your whole house. I'll jump up and down on your front lawn bare naked.

MAGGIE: Good, I hope he freezes his nuts off.

SARA: Maybe we should open the window.

MAGGIE: No, let him get pneumonia.

(SARA opens the window a crack. BOB hands her a note.)

BOB: Maggie, please!

(MAGGIE runs to the window and closes it.)

SARA: Maybe you should read this.

(MAGGIE reads it. BOB watches anxiously from the window. MAGGIE goes to the window, opens it, shoves the note in BOB's smiling mouth and shuts it again.)

BOB: Maggie, give me a chance!

SARA: What did he do?

MAGGIE: He told Luke I was a slut. That's why Luke thought he could come on to me.

SARA: Do you really think that would make a difference to Luke?

MAGGIE: I thought he was my friend.

SARA: Then hear him out.

(Pause. SARA opens the window.)

BOB: Can I come in? *(He crawls in.)* Thank you. I'm freezing. Howya doing, Sara?

SARA: Don't worry about me.

BOB: Maggie?

(MAGGIE won't look at him.)

Maggie?

(He moves around to see her face but she turns again.)

Maggie—Luke was being really weird, he started saying things about you and me, that he heard we were more than just friends. I didn't deny it. I know it was stupid but I was scared. I must've been afraid he'd think I was a loser. But all I proved was I really am a loser.

MAGGIE: You can say that again.

BOB: I really am a loser.

MAGGIE: Will you shut up, Bob!

BOB: Well, I am. My only friend and I eat her lunch and make like I was boinking her ...

MAGGIE: Bob!

SARA: ... I gotta go.

MAGGIE: You want us to come with you?

SARA: No.

MAGGIE: Sara—be careful.

SARA: Right.

MAGGIE: We're here if you need us.

BOB: For sure.

SARA: Thanks.

(SARA exits.)

BOB: What's going on?

MAGGIE: I don't know.

BOB: Is she gonna break up with him?

MAGGIE: I don't know.

BOB: She'll never do it, she's addicted to that guy.

MAGGIE: It won't be easy for her either way.

BOB: That's for sure ... just what did Luke say we did together, anyway?

MAGGIE: He said we did it in the washroom.

BOB: You and me? In the washroom? Did it?

MAGGIE: Yeah.

BOB: What was it like?

MAGGIE: How am I supposed to know?

BOB: Maybe I was asleep. If you lose your virginity sleepwalking, does it count?

MAGGIE: No, because it never happened.

BOB: He asked if we were an item and if you were wild. That's all. Where did he get this washroom stuff?

MAGGIE: It must be a rumour. It's gossip.

BOB: About us? They really gossip about us?

MAGGIE: I guess so.

BOB: Wow. Would we have done it in the boys' or the girls'?

MAGGIE: Bob.

BOB: I was just curious. I think I'd rather do it in the girls' 'cause it's cleaner.

MAGGIE: That's what you think!

(MAGGIE hits BOB with a pillow. They hear Maggie's MOTHER's voice. They freeze. BOB assumes they're in trouble.)

MOTHER: Maggie?

MAGGIE: Yeah, Mom?

MOTHER: Could you get me another drink, darling?

MAGGIE: Go back to sleep, Mom.

(Pause. MAGGIE listens. BOB is shocked. MAGGIE shrugs.)

MAGGIE: Perfect life, huh?

BOB: I didn't know, I—

MAGGIE: Forget it. See ya tomorrow.

BOB: Maggie, we gotta talk about this.

MAGGIE: Don't worry about it.

BOB: Don't worry about it? How can I not worry about it?

MAGGIE: Okay, okay, we'll talk ...

(She indicates that her MOTHER is near.)

... later.

BOB: For sure?

MAGGIE: Yeah.

BOB: Promise?

MAGGIE: ... Promise.

BOB: Scout's Honour?

MAGGIE: Get outta here!

(BOB exits out the window. MAGGIE watches him go.)

MAGGIE: Okay, Mom, let's get you to bed.

(MAGGIE exits. Music. SARA and LUKE enter from opposite directions.)

LUKE: Hi, baby.

SARA: Hi.

LUKE: It's late.

SARA: Yeah, really late.

LUKE: I was looking for you.

SARA: I figured.

LUKE: Where were you?

SARA: At Maggie's.

LUKE: You were talking to Maggie.

SARA: And Bob.

LUKE: I thought I told you not to talk to that guy.

SARA: I can talk to who I want.

LUKE: You got the hots for him or what?

SARA: We're friends.

LUKE: I can't trust you, can I? I can't trust you at all.

SARA: What are you talking about? You're the one who's always screwing up, not me.

LUKE: Come on, you're over-reacting.

SARA: No.

LUKE: Why are you so paranoid? What did they say to you?

SARA: Nothing, they didn't say anything to me!

LUKE: Then don't be so emotional.

SARA: Don't tell me how to be. We're through.

LUKE: What?

SARA: I don't want to see you anymore.

LUKE: You're kidding.

SARA: No.

LUKE: You're making a big deal out of nothing.

SARA: It's not just what you did to Maggie. It's what you do to me.

LUKE: What have I done to you?

SARA: You don't let me move, you don't let me breathe. You're jealous of all my friends, you put me down all the time and when that's not enough, you beat me up.

LUKE: Something goes wrong and you want to run. You don't care about me at all.

(We hear the voices of MARY and JOE, off.)

JOE: You don't love me.

MARY: Yes I do, Joe.

LUKE: You're just not willing to try, you never loved me.

SARA: ... I did, Luke. I do. But I'm not gonna let you hurt me anymore.

MARY: What's wrong, Joe?

LUKE: I'm not hurting you, you're hurting me.

JOE: What are you pulling on me?

SARA: I'm just telling you the truth.

MARY: Nothing, it's the truth.

LUKE: No, you're lying, you're lying like you always lie.

JOE: You're a lying bitch!

SARA: You're turning out just like your old man.

MARY: Relax, Joe.

LUKE: What's that supposed to mean?

JOE: Shut up.

SARA: You know exactly what I mean.

MARY: I'm sorry, Joe.

LUKE: You shut up about my father! You don't know a thing about my father!

MARY: No, Joe, don't.

SARA: Luke—

JOE: Liar!

LUKE: You filthy liar!

> (*LUKE hits SARA. JOE hits MARY. Pause. Both women are down. We see JOE and MARY on the screen.*)

LUKE: Sara. Are you okay? Sara?

JOE: You okay, Mary?

MARY: I'll be fine.

SARA: I'm still alive.

LUKE: I'm sorry, I'm so sorry.

JOE: Why do you provoke me?

MARY: I didn't mean to.

LUKE: You get me so mad.

SARA: I know. You can't help yourself.

MARY: I'm sorry I upset you.

LUKE: Something snapped, you know what I mean?

LUKE and JOE: I swear it'll never happen again.

MARY: I know, Joe.

SARA: Liar.

LUKE: I swear it.

JOE: You'll always stay with me?

MARY: I'll never leave you, Joe.

SARA: No.

LUKE: I need you.

MARY: I'll take care of you.

SARA: No.

MARY: Where else can I go?

SARA: It doesn't have to be like this.

LUKE: No one knows you like me.

SARA: I have friends.

MARY: I only have you.

> *(JOE and MARY embrace.)*

SARA: I have friends!

> *(JOE and MARY fade from screen.)*

LUKE: If you leave me, I'll die.

SARA: That's your choice.

LUKE: I'll kill myself. I'll blow my brains out.

SARA: I know how to hurt myself too, dammit, but you're not doing
it for me!

LUKE: You'll never get rid of me. Never.

SARA: Just watch. Watch me!

> *(SARA starts to go.)*

LUKE: Sara, stop.

> *(SARA stops.)*

Look in my eyes.

> *(SARA looks in LUKE's eyes.)*

Our souls are crossed. They can't ever split apart. You need me. Feel it.

(Pause.)

SARA: Goodbye, Luke.

(SARA turns and goes.)

LUKE: Sara, come back here. I'm gonna find you. You can't walk away from me that easy. I'll get you! You're mine! Sara!

(Pause. SARA goes to MAGGIE.)

SARA: Maggie ... I think—it's been a whole month and no phone calls, no letters, no following me in his car. I didn't know if I could make it. But I think it might be over.

MAGGIE: Me too.

SARA: I don't have to be afraid anymore.

BOB: *(To audience.)* It wasn't easy and took a long time, we had to get some help, including the cops.

(MAGGIE and SARA run into the washroom, laughing.)

MAGGIE: Did he see us? Did he see us?

SARA: Mr. Fritter? Are you kidding? That guy sleeps with his eyes open. Gotta light?

MAGGIE: Sorry.

SARA: ... He's so filled with pain.

MAGGIE: Mr. Fritter?

SARA: No, Luke.

(They look at each other.)

It's okay. I'm not going back.

MAGGIE: It's up to him now.

BOB: *(To audience.)* So now Sara and me are going out, we're really in love, I think we might even end up getting married.

SARA: *(To MAGGIE.)* I like being single. No boyfriends for me right now.

BOB: *(To audience.)* Okay, so we're just friends, she's not going out with anybody now. The truth is, it took me a long time to realize how good I had it, but then I had to face it. So Maggie and I are going out now and we regularly visit the girls' washroom—

SARA: *(To MAGGIE.)* Where's Ricky taking you tonight?

MAGGIE: *(To SARA.)* To a Green Party rally.

BOB: Okay, okay, so Maggie's going out with somebody else now. And me? I'm all alone.

SARA and MAGGIE: Bob!

BOB: Except for two true blue friends.

SARA and MAGGIE: Will you move it!

BOB: I'm coming! I'm coming!

　　(The End.)

Vancouver-based writer and director **Dennis Foon** is known both nationally and internationally for his contribution to innovative theatre for young people. In 1989 he received the International Arts for Young Audiences Award in recognition of his work. His many plays, which have been produced extensively throughout Canada and the world (translated into French, Danish, Hebrew and Cantonese), include *The Short Tree and the Bird that Could Not Sing* (Chalmers Award), *Invisible Kids* (British Theatre Award), *New Canadian Kid, Mirror Game, Skin* (Chalmers Award and a Governor General's nomination), and *War*. His award-winning screenplay "Little Criminals", was produced by CBC TV as a television feature film. Dennis is co-founder of Vancouver's Green Thumb Theatre where he was Artistic Director from 1975 to 1987.